WEST AFRICAN MYTHS

By Jen Green

Gareth Stevens
Publishing

Please visit our Web site www.garethstevens.com. For a free color catalog of all our high-quality books, call toll free 1-800-542-2595 or fax 1-877-542-2596.

Library of Congress Cataloging-in-Publication Data
Giles, Bridget, 1970-
    West African myths / Bridget Giles.
      p. cm. -- (Myths from around the world)
    Includes index.
    ISBN 978-1-4339-3536-7 (library binding) -- ISBN 978-1-4339-3537-4 (pbk.)
    1. Mythology, West African--Juvenile literature. 2. Folklore--Africa, West--Juvenile literature. I. Title.
  BL2465.G57 2010
  398.20966--dc22

                                               2009039332

Published in 2010 by
Gareth Stevens Publishing
111 East 14th Street, Suite 349
New York, NY 10003

© 2010 The Brown Reference Group Ltd.

For Gareth Stevens Publishing:
Art Direction: Haley Harasymiw
Editorial Direction: Kerri O'Donnell

For The Brown Reference Group Ltd:
Editorial Director: Lindsey Lowe
Managing Editor: Tim Cooke
Editor: Henry Russell
Children's Publisher: Anne O'Daly
Picture Manager: Sophie Mortimer
Design Manager: David Poole
Designers: Tim Mayer and John Walker
Production Director: Alastair Gourlay

Picture Credits:
Front Cover: Corbis: Seattle Art Museum b; Jupiter Images: PhotoObjects br; Shutterstock: t

Corbis: Atlantide Phototravel/Massimo Borchi; iStock: Bibi57 17; Brasil2 45; Brunette 33r; Grafissimo 24; Alan Tobey 12, 16, 25, 36; Shutterstock: 20; abenda 43; AMA 15; Galyana Andrushko 9t; Attem 8; Mairilo Bertomeu 41; Bullwinkle 35; John Carnemolla 19; Lucian Coman 27; Devi 13; Laszlo Dobos 29; Andreas Gradin 37; Jay Hocking 31; Attila Jandi 21; Arnold John Labrentz 32; Francois Loubser 11; Per Oyvind Mathisen 33l; Gabriel Openshaw 7; Stefanie Mohr Photography 28; Szefei 9b; Alan Tobey 44; Varuka 23

Publisher's note to educators and parents: Our editors have carefully reviewed the Web sites that appear on p. 47 to ensure that they are suitable for students. Many Web sites change frequently, however, and we cannot guarantee that a site's future contents will continue to meet our high standards of quality and educational value. Be advised that students should be closely supervised whenever they access the Internet.

Manufactured in the United States of America
1 2 3 4 5 6 7 8 9 12 11 10   0|50

CPSIA compliance information: Batch #BRW0102GS: For further information contact Gareth Stevens, New York, New York at 1-800-542-2595.

Contents

Introduction

Myths are mirrors of humanity. They reflect the soul of a culture and try to give profound answers in a seemingly mysterious world. They give the people an understanding of their place in the world and the universe.

Found in all civilizations, myths sometimes combine fact and fiction and at other times are complete fantasy.

Every culture has its own myths. Yet, globally, there are common themes, even across civilizations that had no contact with each other. The most common myths deal with the creation of the world or of a particular site, like a mountain or a lake. Other myths deal with the origin of humans or describe the heroes and gods who either made the world inhabitable or who provided humans with something essential, such as the ancient Greek Titan Prometheus, who gave fire, and the Native American Wunzh, who was given divine instructions on cultivating corn. There are also myths about the end of the world, death, and the afterlife.

The origin of evil and death are also common themes. Examples of such myths are the Biblical Eve eating the forbidden fruit and the ancient Greek story of Pandora opening the sealed box. Additionally, there are flood myths, myths about the sun and the moon, and myths of peaceful places of reward, such as heaven or Elysium, and of places of punishment, such as hell or Tartarus. Myths also teach human values, such as courage and honesty.

This volume features some of the most important ancient West African myths. Following each myth is an explanation of how the myth related to real life. A glossary at the end of the book identifies the major mythological and historical characters and explains many cultural terms.

Mythology of West Africa

The myths of West Africa are as diverse and varied as its people. Thousands of languages are spoken in the region, and many different religions are followed. Each group of people has its own myths, and the details of the stories can vary

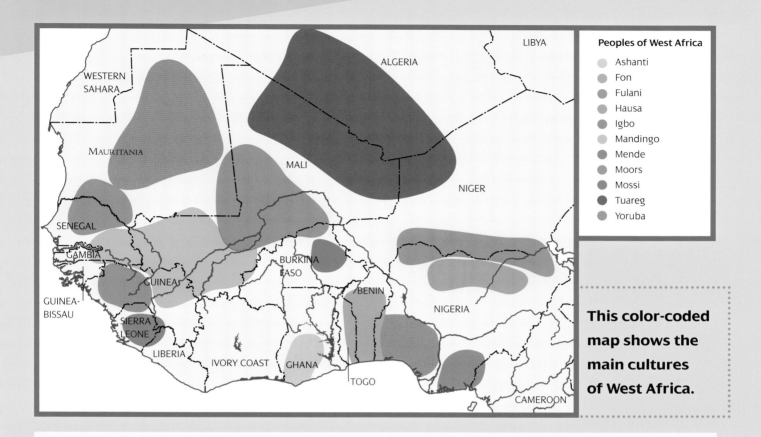

Peoples of West Africa

- Ashanti
- Fon
- Fulani
- Hausa
- Igbo
- Mandingo
- Mende
- Moors
- Mossi
- Tuareg
- Yoruba

This color-coded map shows the main cultures of West Africa.

within groups depending who is retelling them. Myths also change over the centuries as the culture that created them evolves. Some stories spread to other regions and were adopted by different ethnic groups, each of which adapted them for its own purposes.

Studying the myths of West Africa can reveal some surprises. To many people, myths are typically the stories of religions whose followers are long dead. Yet many West African myths are integral parts of modern faiths, such as the Yoruba and Igbo religions, whose followers still number in the many thousands.

Over 1,000 years ago, many West Africans began adopting Islam and Christianity. Traditional African religions are still widely followed, however, often alongside the world faiths. Many African myths reflect this diversity, with elements of Christianity and Islam interwoven with native religions.

African myths have spread around the globe and spawned new traditions, especially in North America and South America. They are no longer only about religion and spiritual beliefs. They are told to entertain and educate people in history and standards of acceptable behavior.

Iyadola's Babies

People's myths explain the world around them. West Africa is a region of diverse peoples, cultures, languages, and religions. This Igbo myth relates how all people were created by Iyadola, the Earth Mother.

In the beginning, there was only sky and barren earth. Nyame, who is also called the Sky God, was lonely in the clouds. One day, he filled a calabash (a container made from a gourd) with plants and animals, then ripped a huge hole in the sky. Nyame lowered the calabash containing his creations to Earth, where they flourished and multiplied. From then on, the Sky God no longer felt lonely, with lions, elephants, monkeys, birds, and other animals for him to watch on Earth.

Inside Nyame lived two spirit people, a man and a woman. They, too, liked to watch events unfold beneath them and would creep to Nyame's lip to peer out of his mouth. One day Nyame sneezed and the pair flew out of his mouth, landing on the ground below. Unable to return to the sky, they made themselves at home. The man learned how to kill animals with sharpened sticks. He left the woman, Iyadola, at home while he went hunting.

Iyadola was lonely. One day, she had an idea. "If I find clay and make some little people and bake them in the fire, they could be our children." The next day, she and her husband made a batch of little clay children and placed them in the warm embers of a fire. Suddenly, they heard the Sky God crashing through the forest. Afraid that their creations would anger him, Iyadola and her husband plucked the clay children from the fire and hid them. When Nyame reached their clearing, he asked what the fire was for. "To keep us warm," they replied.

Starting the Races

The Sky God was suspicious, but he left them alone for the time being. Iyadola and her husband made several more batches of clay children that day, but Nyame kept returning without warning when they tried to bake them. Some batches had to be taken out of the fire before they were ready, and others were

overcooked. When night fell and Nyame returned to the sky, Iyadola laid her creations out on the forest floor. Some of the children were white because they were not cooked properly. Others had been burned black. Some were yellow, brownish red, or pink. Iyadola breathed life into her children. They opened their eyes, wriggled their feet, and were soon playing in the forest. Iyadola, who is also known as the Earth Mother, was never lonely again.

Africans are not a single people but a wide range of nationalities, ethnicities, and even colors.

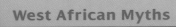
Languages and Peoples

West Africa is a region of great diversity, both culturally and linguistically. Around 700 different languages are spoken in West Africa, more than in any other region of comparable size in the world.

West Africa, where the Igbo myth of Iyadola and her clay children originates, takes up a vast chunk of the world's second-largest continent (see the map on page 5). It includes Mauritania, Mali, Niger, Cameroon, and all the countries that border them. The landscape of the region is highly varied and features deserts, semideserts, grasslands, forests, highlands, and mangrove swamps.

Diversity

The people of West Africa, like Iyadola's clay children, are even more diverse than the landscape. It is common to divide African peoples into "tribes," but this term is not really appropriate for groups of people that number in the millions and have histories stretching back thousands of years. People are divided into these so-called tribes, or ethnic groups, according to the language they speak, the history they share, and often also the religion they practice. Because all these features change over the centuries, ethnic groups are flexible concepts that are often more recent than people realize.

Most West Africans are black but an important minority are not. They include Arabs from North Africa and farther afield, as well as Europeans and Asians.

Mangrove swamps are abundant along the coasts and great rivers of West Africa.

The Moors are West African peoples of Arab origin. They sometimes pitch camps like this in the Sahara Desert.

Many black Africans, such as the Fang of Gabon, speak Bantu languages that probably originated in the great forests between the Niger and Congo rivers.

Many other West Africans speak languages described as semi-Bantu, including Yoruba and Ashanti. The Bambara, Malinke, Mandingo, and Mende people all speak Mande languages. Others, such as the Hausa of northern Nigeria, speak languages that are related to East African and Middle Eastern languages.

The Fulani, the Moors of Mauritania, and the Tuareg, who, respectively, have African, Arabic, and Berber ancestors, speak languages that reflect their history.

Although most West Africans still make their living by farming or raising animals, today many people of the region live in towns and cities, and work in offices, shops, and modern industries. Farmers and nomads trade goods, and it is often women who dominate the markets in modern West Africa.

Lost and Found

The Dausi epic poems are sung and narrated by the griots (storytellers) of the Soninke people. They tell the part mythical, part factual history of the city of Wagadu.

Like all epic poems, the Dausi are full of stories about heroes and heroines, great battles, and outstanding deeds. The Dausi, which were first sung to a prince by a bird, reveal how Wagadu was lost to humanity four times. The first time, the city disappeared to punish the vanity of the king and his oldest son. Wagadu later reappeared but was lost again through falsehood, then greed, and finally dissension.

Wagadu's first reappearance was thanks to Lagarre, the youngest son of an old and infirm Soninke king called Mama Dinga. The king declared that if the great war drum, Tabele, were found, Wagadu would become visible again. Tabele had been stolen by jinn (genies) and tied to the sky. Fooled into thinking that Lagarre was his eldest son, the near-blind Mama Dinga told Lagarre that if he washed in the contents of nine magical jars, he would understand the language of the jinn and all the animals.

Lagarre did as his father instructed. Soon afterward, a jinni appeared who told the prince to visit an ancient lizard in the forest. The lizard sent him to the jackal, who sent him to the buzzard, Kiloko. After Lagarre had fed Kiloko for 10 days, the bird was strong enough to wrench Tabele from the sky and bring it to Lagarre. When Lagarre beat the great war drum, Wagadu appeared before him.

Sacrificial Bargain

In front of the city's gates lay a mighty snake called Bida. Kiloko had warned Lagarre that Bida would expect to be given 10 maidens every year in return for making it rain gold three times a year. Lagarre faced the coiled serpent and made a new bargain with him—one maiden a year for three rainfalls of gold.

Bida agreed, and the ritual sacrifice to the serpent continued for many years until it became the turn of Sia Jatta Bari, the most beautiful of all Soninke maidens.

The buzzard Kiloko features prominently in this story of the city of Wagudu.

Sia was in love with a nobleman called Mamadi Sefe Dekote. He swore that Wagadu would rot before he let Sia be killed by Bida. On the day of the sacrifice, Mamadi sharpened his sword until it could split a grain of wheat. The people of Wagadu led Sia to the well where Bida lived. As usual, Bida raised his head from the well three times. On the third time, Mamadi cut off the serpent's head with one stroke of his sword. As Bida's head flew through the air, the snake cried: "For seven years, seven months, and seven days, Wagadu will be without its golden rain." Bida's curse angered the people of Wagadu, and they turned on Mamadi. Mamadi swept Sia onto his horse and rode away with her to safety. Bida's head landed far away to the south, where it became a source of much gold.

Oral History

Griots are more than professional storytellers. They also record historical facts. They do so not in books but by narrating stories or performing songs, such as the Dausi, which are passed down from generation to generation.

The tale of how Lagarre revealed the city of Wagadu originated long before cultures began writing down stories. In West Africa, tales were and still are preserved by word of mouth, which is termed oral history. Scientific studies of ancient artifacts, languages, and documents such as traveler's accounts have proved many oral accounts to be accurate. Oral history includes praise songs, epic poems, riddles, proverbs, children's rhymes, folktales, fables, legends, and myths. Praise songs relate the exploits of local or national heroes, including politicians today. Legends and myths explain the sometimes partly factual origins of people, kings, dynasties, cities, and kingdoms.

Epic poems are long stories on a grand scale. People the world over have epic poems. The ancient Greeks had the *Iliad* and the *Odyssey*, and the Anglo-Saxons had *Beowulf*. It was only recently that scholars recognized Africa had such narratives, too. More than 1,700 years ago, the Soninke people established a kingdom based around the city of Wagadu. It grew into an empire that became known as Ghana, which was also the king's title. The history of this state is recounted in the Dausi.

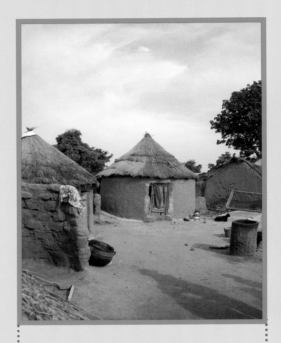

Griots traveled through villages such as this to spread the stories that became part of the common culture of the West African peoples.

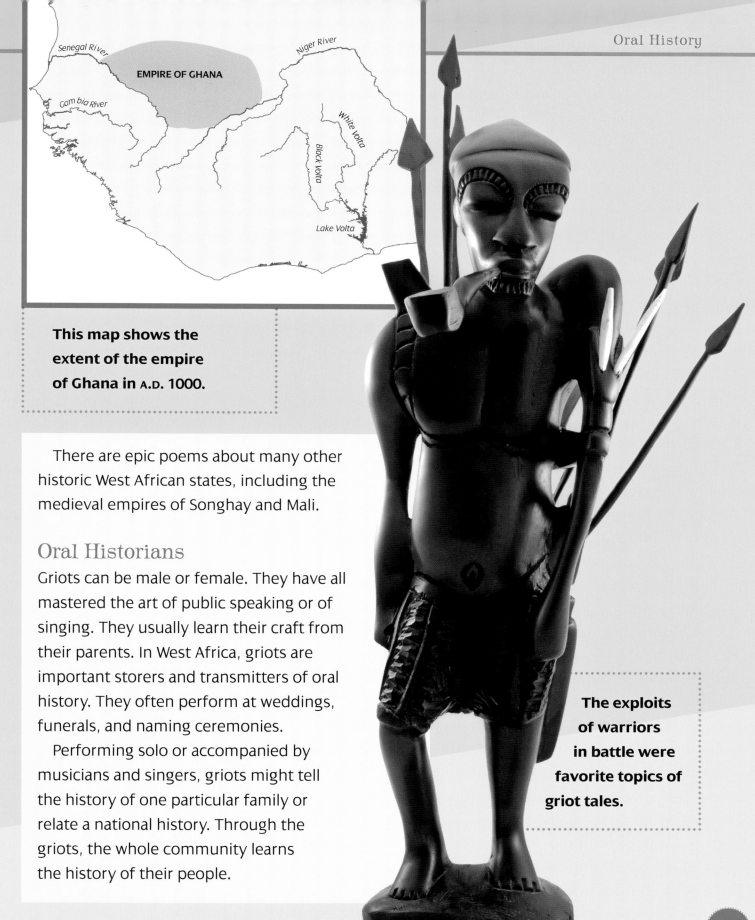

EMPIRE OF GHANA

Senegal River

Gambia River

Niger River

White Volta

Black Volta

Lake Volta

This map shows the extent of the empire of Ghana in A.D. 1000.

There are epic poems about many other historic West African states, including the medieval empires of Songhay and Mali.

Oral Historians

Griots can be male or female. They have all mastered the art of public speaking or of singing. They usually learn their craft from their parents. In West Africa, griots are important storers and transmitters of oral history. They often perform at weddings, funerals, and naming ceremonies.

Performing solo or accompanied by musicians and singers, griots might tell the history of one particular family or relate a national history. Through the griots, the whole community learns the history of their people.

The exploits of warriors in battle were favorite topics of griot tales.

Seven Sons for Seven Virgins

Tuareg traders once dominated large parts of the Sahara Desert. They also roamed the dry grasslands of the Sahel—the semideserts of northern Niger and Mali in West Africa and southern Algeria and Libya in North Africa.

Although the Tuareg have been Muslim for many centuries, they have myths that date from before Muhammad (A.D. 570–632), the founder of Islam. These ancient Tuareg myths tell of spirit founders. Thousands of years ago, a people called the Gaawo lived in a vast desert. One year, the Gaawo were beaten in battle by a foreign tribe. Every year following their defeat, the Gaawo had to pay tribute to their conquerors by sending them seven virgins.

Usually, the seven Gaawo virgins were sent on their long journey across the desert alone, but one year the elders decided that a wise man should accompany the young women. Spirits called jinn (genies) lived in the desert, and they might harm the virgins before they completed their journey. The Gaawo feared that if the virgins did not reach their destination safely, there might be harsh reprisals from their rulers. The man the elders chose to travel with the women was an old marabout, a Muslim holy man of great wisdom and learning.

Miracle in the Desert

Riding on camels, the group set out early one morning. After a long day's journey, they reached a valley. On the valley floor, they saw a patch of green among the sand dunes and dry plains. Palm trees and figs grew in the lush oasis, which was watered by a small body of water. The marabout told the others to wait for him on the valley ridge while he made sure it was safe. He found traces of jinni in the valley, and rushed back to inform the Gaawo virgins, but he arrived too late. The women had already pitched their tent by the oasis on the water's edge and fallen asleep.

During the night, a jinni named Maghegh rose like a dark mist from the water and entered the bodies of the women. When they woke, they were all pregnant with sons.

Instead of completing their journey, the women stayed at the oasis until the children were born and then raised them there with the help of their learned guide. The boys' father, Maghegh, met them in the desert from time to time and taught them magical skills. The boys grew up to be brave and resourceful warriors. They fought and worked for local chiefs, who rewarded them with wives. In this way, the descendants of Maghegh's seven virgin "wives" prospered and grew in number, forming the main clans of the Tuareg.

The Sahara Desert formed an unexplored and mysterious backdrop to life in West Africa.

Nomads in the Sahara

In size and difficulty of crossing, the Sahara Desert has been compared to an ocean. Yet it has not prevented West Africans, such as the Tuareg, from building links with the wider world.

The story of Maghegh's wives places the origin of the Tuareg in a remote oasis in the Sahara. For thousands of years, the Tuareg and other nomadic peoples have lived and worked in the desert, trading goods from north to south. The Tuareg's real ancestors, the Berbers, were the first people to inhabit North Africa.

By the time the region was conquered by Arabs in the eighth century A.D., the Berbers had broken into different groups, including the Tuareg, who gradually moved southward. By the twentieth century, Tuaregs lived in Mali and Niger in West Africa, and in Algeria and Libya in North Africa. Today the Tuareg, who speak a Berber language, include black Africans and Arabs among their ancestors.

Traditional Life

The Tuareg bred camels, cattle, goats, and sheep. They were nomads who moved from one water hole or pasture to the next to feed and water their animals.

Nomadic herdsmen tether their fully-laden camels in the Sahara Desert near the modern city of Timbuktu, Mali.

SULTAN OF AIR

While most Africans benefited by controlling the trade depots on the edge of the Sahara Desert, the trade routes themselves were run by the Tuareg. Huge caravans of Tuaregs headed north with gold, slaves, ebony, and ivory. They came back with grain, weapons, glass, cotton, and salt.

To prevent disputes between their seven clans, the Tuareg elected an overall leader. Known as the Sultan of Air and based in Agadez (a region of modern Niger), he governed an area that, by the nineteenth century, stretched north to Libya and south to Nigeria.

Most Tuareg myths of origin involve women as the founding ancestors. Tuaregs trace their descent through their mothers. Tuareg property and possessions are normally held in the woman's name. A Tuareg man will identify himself as the son of a woman from a certain clan.

Tuaregs wore loose, flowing clothes that prevented them losing too much water in sweat and kept sunlight off their skin. Tuareg men wore long veils called *tagelmusts* wrapped around their heads and over their faces. These veils were usually colored a deep blue with indigo dye. Some of the dye would rub off on the wearers' faces, giving the Tuareg their nickname of "Blue Men." It was considered rude for a man to show his face. Unlike many other Muslim women, Tuareg women were not expected to cover their faces.

A herdsman wears the typical blue headdress of the Tuareg people.

The Emperor and the Magician

At the start of the nineteenth century, Seku Ahmadu (1775–1844) founded the Muslim state of Macina, located in modern Mali. One of his aims was to bring more converts to Islam.

Seku Ahmadu wanted to wipe out all religions except Islam. Although many of the people living in his region—the Bambara and the Songhay, for example—were already Muslim, they still consulted priests associated with ancient local water spirits called jinn (genies).

Seku Ahmadu declared that priests who did not turn to Islam would be executed unless they could prove that the powers they claimed were real. One priest, Waada Samba, was known far and wide as a man of great powers. He lived to the north of Seku Ahmadu's capital on an island in a great pool. Stories of the miracles Waada performed reached Ahmadu, who sent an impressive cavalry to collect the old man.

Ahmadu ordered his servants to catch a guinea fowl (an African pheasant) and enclose it in a lidded pot so that no one could tell what was inside. Then he summoned all the marabouts (Muslim holy men) and Waada and his followers. Ahmadu told the assembled wise men, "Use your powers to divine what is in this pot; he who lies will have his throat cut." The marabouts were the first to try. After much discussion and divining, one of them said, "The animal has four paws." Another added, "And large ears." A third concluded, "It's a hare!" Seku Ahmadu was very disappointed with their answers, but he remained calm and gave no sign.

Diplomatic Solution

Waada Samba danced around the pot, until he fell into a trance. Half awake and half unconscious, he communicated with his jinni. Waada emerged from the trance to declare forcefully, "The animal has two

feet, wings, and is black with white spots. It's a guinea fowl."

Seku Ahmadu was in a dilemma. If the people of his new state learned that the marabouts had been outwitted by a local priest, they were unlikely to abandon their old beliefs. Ahmadu prayed to Allah (God), "Make this priest into a liar so that light can triumph over darkness."

Seku Ahmadu lifted the lid off the pot and out jumped a small hare. The animal

In addition to being an important souce of food, guinea fowl are used as guards because they gabble when disturbed.

skittered across the ground for several yards, then transformed back into a guinea fowl and flew away. It was decided that, although the local priest had told the truth, Allah was always right.

Along the Niger

The Niger River has been called the Nile of West Africa for its fertile shores and important historical role. Many powerful nations arose on its banks, including two of the largest ever in Africa—Mali and Songhay.

Macina, where Seku Ahmadu converted his people to Islam, lay in Mali. Mali was one of Africa's most powerful empires. Its wealth was based on the fertile farmland and easy transport provided by the Niger River. The Niger rises in Guinea then passes in a gigantic arc through modern Mali, Niger, and Nigeria to the Atlantic Ocean. At 2,600 miles (4,200 km), it is the third-longest river in Africa.

For 300 miles (480 km) in central Mali, the river splits into many channels, becoming a network

The Niger River is surrounded by rich farmland and provides an important pathway for trade and contact between the peoples of West Africa.

of creeks, swamps, lakes, and pools dotted with sandbanks and islands. This is one of the most fertile regions in Africa. The river itself provided transport links with the gold-producing regions in the forests to the south and with overland trade routes across the Sahara Desert.

Great Powers

A succession of states dominated the Niger River. One of the earliest was the empire of Ghana (see page 12), which controlled the river port of Timbuktu.

A small kingdom called Kangaba was founded along the river around 750 by Mandingo-speaking people. In 1224, all members of the ruling family were killed by Susu invaders. All, that is, except one crippled prince called Sundiata, who was spared because he was not considered a threat. This was a mistake. Sundiata, the "Lion of Mali," conquered the Susu and what was left of the empire of Ghana, and created the empire of Mali.

Mali grew rich by controlling the goldfields in the south and the trade routes to the north. It reached the height of its power under Mansa Musa (around 1264–1337) but then quickly declined.

Mali was succeeded by the Songhay empire. The Songhay capital was Gao, a city on the Niger River. Sunni Ali (1464–1492) and his successor, Askia Muhammad (1493–1528), made Songhay one of the largest and most powerful empires the world had ever seen. The Songhay empire ended when it was conquered by Morocco in 1591.

Islam is one of the main religions of West Africa. Mansa Musa was a Muslim. This is a mud mosque in Djenne, Mali.

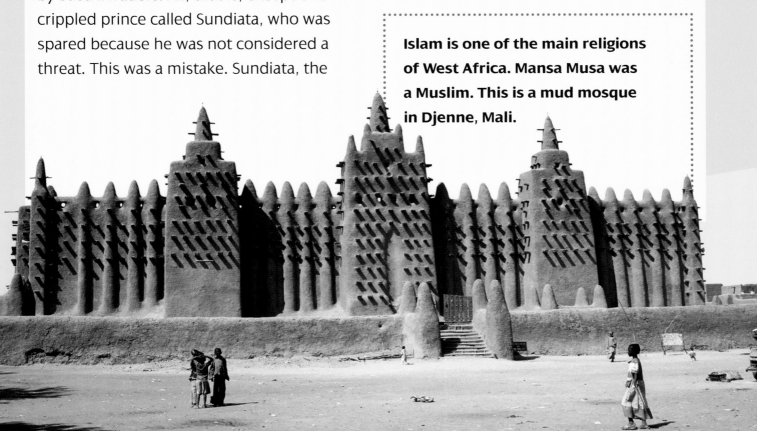

Two Brothers Quarrel

The Fon people of Benin worship a host of vodun *(gods) and a supreme god, Mawu-Lisa. This myth explains how Sagbata came to reign over the earth* vodun *and Sogbo over the* vodun *of thunder, lightning, rain, and storms.*

After Mawu-Lisa created the universe, she told her sons, Sagbata and Sogbo, to rule the world on her behalf. The brothers argued constantly until Sagbata, the elder, left the sky and went down to Earth. Mawu-Lisa then decided to make Sagbata the lord of all her wealth on Earth and to put Sogbo in charge of thunder and lightning.

When Sagbata moved to Earth, he packed many precious treasures in his travel bag but left water and fire behind because they would have soaked or burned everything else. The journey to Earth was difficult, and Sagbata realized he would never be able to return home.

With Sagbata out of the way, Sogbo could now do whatever he wanted in the sky. To prove that he was now more powerful than Sagbata, he stopped the rain from falling on Earth.

The people on Earth had made Sagbata their king but now regretted that decision. "As long as you have been king, there has been no rain. Our crops won't grow, and our animals can't eat or drink. We are dying," they complained. Sagbata assured them it would soon rain, but the drought continued for three years.

Sagbata learned of two sky spirits who had come to Earth to teach *fa* (divination). When someone wanted to ask the gods a question, the diviners would throw seeds of prophecy on the ground and read the answer in the patterns formed. Sagbata summoned the diviners. He told them how he had left water behind but now needed it for life on Earth. The diviners told Sagbata that, if he wanted the rains to return, he would have to make friends with his brother.

Reconciliation

Sagbata did not know what to do. He could not meet with his brother, because Sogbo lived in the sky. The diviners told him to summon Wututu, Sogbo's messenger bird, to take a message to Sogbo.

Sagbata summoned Wututu and told the bird that he would let Sogbo rule his part of the universe if Sogbo allowed the rains to fall once more. Wututu flew up into the heavens to speak with Sogbo.

When Sogbo heard the message, he was very pleased. "Tell my brother," he said to the bird, "that, although he is the elder, he was foolish to leave behind the two things that power the universe—fire and water. Nevertheless, I accept his offer." Before Watutu had even reached Earth, it began to rain. Sogbo and Sagbata have remained friends ever since.

The coming of rain is a cause for celebration in West Africa. Its absence causes droughts, which make the crops fail and cause famine.

23

Voodoo and Slavery

Today African influences exist throughout the Americas, one result of the inhuman slave trade. In Brazil and the islands of the Caribbean, people follow religions that are clearly derived from Fon and Yoruba beliefs.

Throughout the world, belief systems help people to explain nature and the universe. In West Africa, the vital importance of the weather inspired the story of Sagbata and Sogbo. These deities held prime positions in the Fon religion.

From the sixteenth century to the nineteenth century, more than six million slaves were shipped from the west coast of Africa to the Americas. They took their religious belief systems with them.

The journey from Africa was horrifying. Hundreds of people were crammed into leaky vessels, and many died during the perilous Atlantic crossing. Those who survived were bought and sold like cattle and forced to spend the rest of their lives working for white owners.

Slavery and an internal slave trade had existed in West Africa for centuries, but never before had so many people been victimized. The lucrative trade lured some Africans into supplying slaves. Wars were increasingly waged to gain captives, who were sold to slave traders at the coast.

Practicing Old Beliefs

African slaves were forced to abandon their cultural practices, but in secret they kept hold of their religious beliefs. Over the centuries, these beliefs merged with other religions. Haitian voodoo, for

Africans on slave ships were treated as cargo. Many died on the voyage to the New World.

example, is based on the Fon religion. Many Haitians worship gods called loa, who often relate directly to Fon *vodun*. Legba and Sogbo (see box) exist in both Haiti and Benin, where the Fon live.

The word *voodoo* has negative meanings in English. This is because the slaves were forced to practice their religion in secret, and many white people feared African rituals that they did not understand. The wooden figures that Fon people used to communicate with their *vodun* were labeled fetishes or idols by the whites, because Europeans thought the carvings themselves were the Fon's gods. These figures were banned, but the slaves made smaller replicas out of cloth that they could easily hide. This is the innocent origin of so-called voodoo dolls.

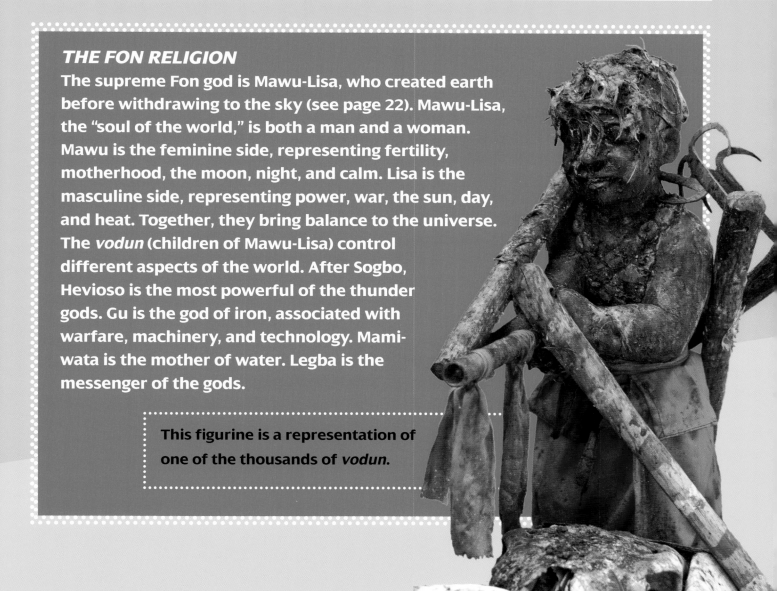

THE FON RELIGION

The supreme Fon god is Mawu-Lisa, who created earth before withdrawing to the sky (see page 22). Mawu-Lisa, the "soul of the world," is both a man and a woman. Mawu is the feminine side, representing fertility, motherhood, the moon, night, and calm. Lisa is the masculine side, representing power, war, the sun, day, and heat. Together, they bring balance to the universe. The *vodun* (children of Mawu-Lisa) control different aspects of the world. After Sogbo, Hevioso is the most powerful of the thunder gods. Gu is the god of iron, associated with warfare, machinery, and technology. Mami-wata is the mother of water. Legba is the messenger of the gods.

This figurine is a representation of one of the thousands of *vodun*.

Anansi and the Rubber Man

In the forested West African state of Ghana, stories are told about the spider Anansi, a famous trickster whose exploits are now known as far afield as the Caribbean and North America.

Anansi the Spider is cunning, but in this famous story he is outwitted and made to look foolish.

Anansi was very lazy. The people of his village worked hard to grow peanuts, but not Anansi. Every day, he got up at noon, ate his breakfast, and then left the house. "I'm going to our farm," he would lie to his wife before spending the afternoon lounging under a tree.

When it was time to plant new crops, Anansi's wife was worried because her husband had not bought any seeds. Eventually, when he could delay planting no longer, Anansi asked his wife to visit the market and buy some nuts for him. The next day, Anansi made a big fuss about taking the nuts to his farm. He did not plant the nuts but spent the day under his favorite tree eating them.

Anansi finished the whole sack of nuts without planting a single one.

For a while, things continued as normal. Anansi would rise at midday, eat his breakfast, then "go to the farm." Then harvest time arrived. The villagers were busy harvesting their nuts. "Where are our nuts?" Anansi's wife asked him. One night, Anansi crept out of his house and headed for the chief's farm. There he filled his bag with nuts and left them under his favorite tree. The next day, he told his wife, "I will harvest our nuts today." His wife was delighted when Anansi returned that evening with a bag full of tasty nuts.

Anansi returned to the chief's farm several nights in a row. The chief's servant realized someone was stealing nuts, so he set a trap. He went to the forest and

tapped a rubber tree, collecting several basins of sticky sap. He used this to make a sticky rubber man, which he planted next to the chief's nut trees.

New World spiders such as this tarantula have helped maintain the modern relevance of the old Anansi legend.

Comeuppance

When Anansi returned to the farm the next night, he was surprised in the darkness by the rubber man. "Who are you?" he cried. There was no reply. "Why don't you answer me?" Anansi swung his fist at the rubber man. It stuck. "Let go of me!" he shouted, and lashed out with his other fist, which also stuck to the rubber man. Anansi tried to push himself off with his feet—they, too, stuck fast.

When the sun rose the next morning, the chief's servant summoned all the villagers to his master's farm, where they saw Anansi the Spider glued to the rubber man. Now they all knew that he was the thief. Ever since then, Anansi and all his spider relatives have hidden away in dark corners because they are too embarrassed to show their faces.

27

Trickster Tales

As well as Anansi the Spider, Tortoise and Hare are popular tricksters in West Africa. Tricksters and other animals appear in fables, which are stories told to teach and entertain.

Nearly all cultures around the world have mythical tricksters, such as Anansi the Spider in West Africa and Coyote for many Native Americans. The Yoruba *orisha* (god) Eshu and the Fon's Legba are contrary characters. If forgotten in a person's prayers, they may take their revenge in unforeseen ways. Yet they are also sought out forprotection, to do good deeds, or to bring harm to a person's enemies.

More commonly, tricksters are animals that people think are clever and cunning, though they may not always approve of the way they behave. Most tricksters are characters in fables. Fables are stories in which good behavior is rewarded and bad behavior is punished. Other animal fables try to explain some of the mysteries of the natural world—how the leopard got his spots, for example.

Trickster tales often provide fables with interesting twists. Although they do not always obey normal rules, tricksters are admired for their ability to beat the odds and outwit much stronger enemies.

The Igbo and Yoruba people of southern Nigeria tell stories of a tortoise trickster. He makes fools of animals much larger than himself, including the elephant. In a world-famous tale that came originally from West Africa, Tortoise challenges Hare to a race, Despite being much slower, Tortoise wins.

The leopard is a powerful figure in the myths of West Africa.

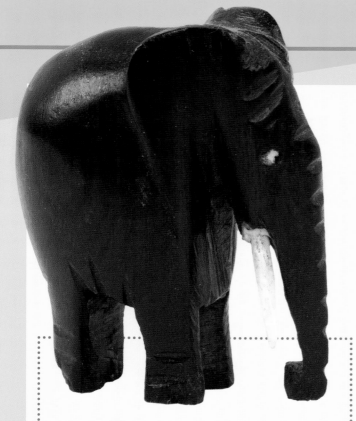

When they came to the Americas, African slaves (see page 24) kept their native languages and cultures alive. Some of their fables were adapted—Hare became Rabbit, for example. Other fables remained much the same—the legends of Anansi the Spider are still very popular in the Caribbean.

Uncle Remus and Brer Rabbit

In 1880, Joel Chandler Harris (1848–1908) published *Uncle Remus: His Songs and His Sayings*. White, Georgia-born Harris wrote the stories after reading about African folklore. Uncle Remus, a wise black slave, told stories about Brer (Brother) Rabbit, who repeatedly outwits the fiercer Brer Fox, Brer Wolf, and Brer Bear.

According to West African legend, the elephant originally had a short nose, but it was stretched into a trunk in a life-or-death struggle with a crocodile.

THE ASHANTI EMPIRE

Though many West African fables tell of spider tricksters, Anansi originally belonged to the Akan-speaking people of Ghana. The most famous Akan people are the Ashanti, whose state became a powerful empire in the eighteenth century. Its wealth was based on trading in gold and slaves, and the well-organized Ashanti army was difficult to defeat. Despite great resistance, the Ashanti were conquered by the British in the early 1900s.

The Ashantihene's (king's) symbol of authority was a golden stool that descended from heaven. Although the Ashantihene was always a man, the queen mother (more often the sister of the king) was an important adviser and had great influence at court.

Sky-Food, Yams, and Cocoyams

Myths of the Igbo people of southeastern Nigeria encourage both individual achievement and responsibility to the community.

The first people, Eri and his wife Namuaku, came from the sky. They were sent down to Earth by the god Chukwu. At that time, most of the land was covered with water, and Eri was forced to perch on a termite mound when he arrived. Disappointed, Eri complained to Chukwu that there was nowhere to go, so Chukwu sent a blacksmith who used his fiery bellows to dry up the land.

Eri and Namuaku made Earth their home, and they soon had children. The family lived on sky-food provided by Chukwu. They ate *azu igwe*, a fish that lived in the back of the sky. Because they ate sky-food, they never needed to sleep.

When Eri died, the food supply dried up. Eri's children did not know how to farm—there were no crops for them to grow anyway. The eldest son, Nri, petitioned Chukwu about their lack of food. Chukwu told him to kill his firstborn son and firstborn daughter and bury them in separate graves. Nri did not want to kill his children, but pleading with Chukwu did not help. With great sadness, Nri killed his eldest daughter and son and buried them as commanded. After three Igbo weeks (12 days), Nri noticed plants sprouting from the graves. Yams grew on the grave of his son and cocoyams on the grave of his daughter. Nri harvested the crops, and when his family ate the new foods, they slept for the first time.

Chukwu then instructed Nri to kill two slaves—a woman and a man—and bury them in separate graves, too. Again, after three Igbo weeks had passed, shoots were spotted sprouting from the graves.

Before the world took on its present form, the only land above the sea was a giant termite mound like this.

This time an oil palm grew on the man's grave and a breadfruit tree on the woman's. Nri's family lived well on their new food supplies.

The Importance of Sharing

Chukwu then commanded Nri to share the crops with the other people who now populated Earth. Nri was not eager to share the fruits of his painful sacrifices. After much debate, Nri and Chukwu reached a compromise. If Nri shared the food, Chukwu would grant him and his descendants privileges over his neighbors. This is how the Nri dynasty was founded. From that day on, the children of Nri—the Umunri—received annual tributes from their neighbors. From Chukwu, they received the *ogwu-ji* (yam medicine), which ensures a good harvest every year for the people of Nri and those who acknowledge their rule.

The Igbo Have No Kings

The Igbo are famous for the flexible, almost democratic nature of their society. Although considered a single tribe, the Igbo were actually a collection of autonomous villages.

A woman proudly parades a huge breadfruit in a West African open-air market.

Following the story of Nri and his crops (see page 30), Igbo men farmed the crops that grew from the graves of Nri's son and male slave—yams and oil palms—and Igbo women farmed the crops that grew from the graves of Nri's daughter and female slave—cocoyams and breadfruit. The men's crops were used in rituals like the yam festival and also as currency.

Igbo Self-Rule

According to a Nigerian saying, "The Igbo have no kings." Although this is not entirely true—the Nri dynasty is not the sole exception—most Igbo lived in highly structured societies that each had policy-making bodies made up of elders, both women and men, age-grade leaders, and heads of titled societies. (An age-grade is a group of men or women who are initiated into adulthood together.) Decisions were made by consensus. Igbo myths reflect this tradition of debate and ability to question authority. Igbo gods can be argued with and challenged.

Status in most Igbo societies was linked to age, wealth, and personal achievement, not birthright. Woman had more rights than in many other civilizations. Village self-rule suffered in the twentieth century when the Igbo were conquered by the British. The British appointed local rulers who used their authority to undermine the complex checks and balances of Igbo politics.

Women were often represented by the Igbo in woodcarvings like this.

Igbo Religion

Each Igbo had his or her own *chi*, a personal divinity or "god within." Today, many Christian Igbo still keep in touch with both their *chi* and the Christian God.

In desert regions, some villages were built underground, out of the harsh glare of the sun.

SUPREME GOD?

Chukwu (see page 30) is often called the supreme god of the Igbo, but this description is based on a partial misunderstanding that arose in the nineteenth century during the European colonization period. Chukwu was originally the chief deity of the Igbo of the Aro region. The Aro Igbo traded widely and spread Chukwu's fame throughout Igbo lands. When the British arrived in West Africa, they heard so much about Chukwu that they assumed he was the supreme god of all the Igbo people. In reality, every Igbo town had its own myth of origin, ancestry, and religious history, and its own chief god.

Prince of Heaven

The spiritual heart of the ancient Yoruba religion has always been the city of Ife, now called Ile-Ife, located in southwest Nigeria. This myth explains why.

In the beginning there was only the sky, the heavens above, and water below. All the gods lived in the heavens, and they were ruled by the wisest and most powerful god, Olorun. The goddess Olokun reigned over the empty waters below heaven.

The gods paid little attention to the water below, but one day a young sky god named Obatala grew bored with the lack of living things there. Knowing that he was the chief god's favorite, Obatala asked Olorun if he could create land over some of the water so that people and animals could roam on it. Olorun allowed Obatala to carry out his plan.

Obatala had no idea how to create land, so he went to see Orunmila (also called Ifa, the god of Divination), who was Prince of Heaven and the eldest son of Olorun. Orunmila could see into the future and told Obatala to find sufficient gold to make a chain long enough to reach down to the waters below.

Joining together all the gold jewelry that belonged to the other gods, Obatala made a chain that he thought was long enough. Next, Orunmila told Obatala to fill a snail's shell with sand and gather a white hen, a black cat, and a palm nut in a bag. After Obatala had done all this, the Prince of Heaven instructed him to carry these things with him down the chain.

Not Far Enough

Orunmila watched over Obatala as he hooked one end of the gold chain to the edge of the sky and lowered the other toward the waters below. Obatala slung the bag over his shoulder and began the descent. He inched his way down the gold chain, but it did not reach the water's surface. It ended far above, and Obatala swung there, unsure of what to do next. Orunmila called out, telling him to empty the sand from the snail's shell. Obatala took the shell from his bag and poured out the sand. Orunmila then told him to release the white hen. Obatala did this, and the bird fluttered down to the sand. The hen scratched at the sand, scattering it all over. Instantly, small heaps of sand turned into hills and large piles of sand made mountains.

Seeds of Life

Obatala jumped onto the newly created land. He took the palm nut from his bag and planted it at the spot where he first landed. Obatala named the spot "Ife," in honor of the god of Divination. Obatala built a house, where he lived with the black cat for company. When Obatala later created children, Ife became the birthplace of humankind.

This tribal mask is thought to represent the Yoruba goddess Olokun, the ruler of the primeval waters.

Yoruba and Its Gods

The Yoruba of southwest Nigeria have been living in towns and cities for more than 1,000 years. They were the first urban people in West Africa.

Today there are more than 20 million Yoruba people living in parts of Benin and Togo as well as southwestern Nigeria. The different Yoruba groups are loosely linked by geography, language, history, and religion. For centuries, the Yoruba have lived in towns and cities. Obatala's Ife (now Ile-Ife), historically the first Yoruba town, could have been founded as early as A.D. 850. It was named for the god of Divination Ifa (or Orunmila, Prince of Heaven; see page 34).

Other towns followed, and each was ruled by a king, called the *alafin* in Oyo and the *oni* in Ife. The *alafins* of Oyo claimed descent from Oduduwa (a son of Olorun, the high god). Though Oyo became an empire, Ife has always remained the center of the Yoruba religion. When an *alafin* of Oyo was enthroned, he had to swear not to attack Ife. One *alafin* who raided Ife for slaves in the 1790s almost began a civil war.

Many Yoruba towns had distinctive wheel-shaped layouts. Some of their citizens were farmers, but many were traders, specialist craft workers, or officials. Several Yoruba cities became flourishing trading and political centers, including Oyo, Ilorin, and Ibadan.

This monument in Lomé, the capital of Togo, celebrates the country's independence from France in 1960.

The fourteenth century was a period of prosperity for Ife, and many works of art were produced for the royal court. The kingdom of Benin, whose citizens were the Edo-speaking Bini, lay to the east. Benin was greatly influenced by Ife. Ife sculptors produced beautiful, realistic human heads in terra-cotta, and Ife metalworkers perfected the art of lost-wax casting to make intricate brass artifacts.

Old and New

Oyo (now Old Oyo) became an empire by conquering neighboring states and dominated a large region from 1650 until 1817, when Ilorin declared independence. Wars between the Yoruba states raged for much of the nineteenth century. Ibadan then took over much of the old Oyo territory.

By 1914, the Yoruba kingdoms had all been defeated by the British and forced to join the Protectorate (colony) of Nigeria.

This figurine was carved by Ife craftsmen in the fourteenth century.

YORUBA GODS

The Yoruba have one overall god, Olorun (or Olodumare), and several hundred deities called *orishas*, who are all extensions of Olorun. The Yoruba religion has no priests. Messages and offerings are delivered to Olorun by Eshu, the messenger god. Eshu is also a trickster, who can cause trouble for those who neglect him or the other *orishas*.

Some *orishas* are older than the earth, while others were once real heroes. Shango, the *orisha* of thunder, was a king of Oyo. Other *orishas* include Olokun (the goddess of waters) and Ogun (the god of iron, war, and technology).

The Mermaid and the Chameleon

This is the Igbo version of a famous myth, common in many different West African civilizations, of the Mermaid, the water goddess, who was outwitted by the Chameleon.

Mermaid, the queen of the oceans, lakes, and seas, felt she should be the supreme god, not Chukwu. The other gods encouraged her vanity and suggested she should arrange a contest with Chukwu. Mermaid was regarded as the most stylish being of all. So she declared a contest to decide whether she or Chukwu was the better dressed. Chukwu agreed to join in.

Impossible Ambitions

On the day of the contest, Chukwu sent Chameleon to fetch the water goddess. Mermaid did not know that Chameleon could change appearance at will. When she arose from her ocean palace, she was horrified to see that Chameleon wore the same outfit as her. Mermaid returned to her palace to change.

More confident, Mermaid returned to her palace gate to meet Chameleon. A great surprise awaited her. Chameleon was again wearing exactly the same outfit as hers. Mermaid rushed inside again to change. This time she put on the most expensive and elaborate clothes she owned; they were covered in rich embroidery and spun from golden thread. To her dismay, Chameleon had changed too, again into identical clothing.

Mermaid then admitted defeat. "If his messenger is so well dressed," she wondered, "how much better dressed must Chukwu be?"

In a similar myth, the Yoruba water goddess, Olokun (see page 34), challenges the supreme god Olorun to a cloth-making contest but is also defeated by the changeable Chameleon.

This myth
was partly
inspired
by the real
chameleon's
ability to change
color to match
its surroundings.

Making Textiles

Making textiles has long been an important economic and artistic activity in West Africa. Today, most working clothes and everyday clothes are imported, but luxury robes for special occasions are still produced locally.

An African woman carries a selection of textiles on her head.

People's clothing says a lot about their social status. The myth of Mermaid being outwitted by Chukwu and Chameleon (see page 38) shows not only that the gods can be vain but also that clothes hold a special place in West African culture. Similarly, a myth of the Mossi people of Sierra Leone relates how their founding ancestor was a weaver who descended to Earth on the threads of his loom.

In spite of competition from mills, handwoven cloth is still valued in West Africa. *Kente*—cloth once worn only by Ashanti kings and now the national dress of Ghana—is distinctive for its intricate patterns made from multicolored threads, often with gold as the dominant color. Yoruba kings wore robes and crowns made from coral beads.

Range of Materials and Styles

The Ewe people of Togo and Ghana made *keta*, a cloth similar to *kente*. They created patterns in the cloth with different-colored warp (lengthwise) and weft (widthwise) threads. *Keta* is woven in narrow strips that are then sewn together to make much wider fabrics. Strips range from less than 0.5 inch (12 mm) wide to nearly a yard (1 m).

Weavers used a variety of threads to make their cloth. Cotton was the most common material. In Nigeria, silk was harvested from the cocoons of wild moths that breed on tamarind trees. The Ashanti used silk unraveled from imported fabrics. Fibers of the raffia palm leaf can be made into threads but are more often kept in loose strips to make costumes such as those worn at masquerades (see pages 44–45). Fulani herders were among the few West African peoples who weaved with wool.

Some materials are not woven at all but made from compressed plant fibers. These include the barkcloth once traded by the Ashanti.

The long, flowing gowns typically worn by West Africans are often decorated with dense borders of embroidery around the neck and cuffs.

The Fon people have perfected the art of appliqué, in which fabric shapes are sewn on to a contrasting background to build up a picture. In the past, appliqué cloths were made to celebrate battles and kings, and to depict Fon gods. Today, they are just as likely to feature social commentary.

This linen cloth is stamped with a typical West African motif showing elephants, trees, and human figures.

Dancing with Spirits

Until recently, most women in Sierra Leone belonged to a Sande society, which prepared girls for adulthood. Myths such as this are told by Sande elders to new recruits.

One year, the Sande society of a big town was holding a masquerade to celebrate a special occasion. Four spirits in the heavens decided that they wanted to attend. Using a long rope, they climbed down to Earth.

The dance lasted four days, and the spirits enjoyed themselves. They met four young women, who liked the spirits a lot. When the masquerade ended, though, it was time for the spirits to return home. The women begged to return with them, but the spirits knew they would not like life in the heavens. They warned them that there would be many sick and poor people. The couples argued all night long. Finally, two of the girls were convinced. They pleaded with their lovers to return, and the spirits said, "We will come back whenever a big dance is held."

The four spirits and the two other women climbed the rope to heaven. The spirit Hawudui's young woman refused to help relieve the suffering of the sick people she met there, while Nyandebo's girlfriend was happy to wash their sores. The women stayed in the heavens until they became homesick, and they told their lovers' friends of their wish to return home. The friends warned the women that they would be tested before they left heaven: "Choose an old, worn box, not a shiny new one," they advised mysteriously.

Nyandebo and Hawudui agreed to let the women return home, but first they told their chief. He summoned the women and spread several boxes on the ground before them. "Choose a box to take with you," the chief ordered. Hawudui's girlfriend chose the shiniest of all the boxes, but Nyandebo's girlfriend chose the oldest and most battered box.

The Consequences

The girls returned home with their prizes. When Nyandebo's friend unpacked her box, she drew out all kinds of riches. She shared her wealth with her whole family and all

In modern Freetown, Sierra Leone, traditional West African religions coexist with the two great world religions of Christianity and Islam.

the town's dancers. They had so many riches that they were able to start trading.

When Hawudui's girlfriend reached her house, she called all her relatives inside. "Shut the doors, and I will show you unimaginable riches," she boasted before asking her father to open the box. As soon as he removed the lid, a leopard leaped out and killed him. It was followed by lions and all kinds of fierce creatures, which ate everyone inside the house, then escaped into the bush.

So it is, thanks to one woman's stubbornness, that there are so many dangerous creatures in the world today. It is also due to the wise behavior of another woman that the Mende became great traders throughout West Africa.

Masks and Masquerades

In West Africa, masked dancers perform at masquerades to entertain and celebrate, as well as to appease or even mock spirits, seek out wrongdoers, and reinforce good behavior.

West Africa is famous for the wide variety of masks, mostly wooden, produced by the sculptors of the region. Few of the masks are older than the nineteenth century, but they are part of a long history of mask making. West African masks vary greatly depending on the area or group. Some peoples make masks shaped like wild animals, while others are more fantastical, with intricate carvings and contorted expressions.

Yet these masks are only one part of an elaborate performance art. They were designed to be worn by dancers wearing costumes at masquerades, often accompanied by musicians, drummers, and singers. Historically, the masquerades were held for a range of reasons, from celebrating victory in battle to honoring the gods. During recent times, the masquerades have been increasingly performed simply to entertain.

The tradition of masked dances is still maintained by the Dogon people of Mali.

A masked dancer can represent a spirit, god, person, or animal. The Bambara people of Mali, for example, wore masks in the shape of antelopes during a masquerade held yearly to honor the god Tyi-wara—half man, half antelope—who taught them how to farm.

West African-style masked dancing thrives today at the carnival in Rio de Janeiro, Brazil.

Range of Meanings

Yoruba Gelede masquerades are performed mainly by men. They acknowledge the power of women to create life and warn against witches.

Masquerades are often associated with particular societies, such as the women's Sande and men's Poro societies of Sierra Leone. New recruits spend several weeks or months in camps in the bush. There they learn the society's history, religion, and codes of conduct, as well as how to diagnose and treat illnesses, farm, weave, spin, dance, and sing.

Sande maskers were almost unique for being women; elsewhere, it is normally men who perform in the masquerades.

Glossary

Anansi the Spider A famous trickster who, in one myth, was caught lying and being lazy.

Askia Muhammad Succeeded Sunni Ali and made Songhay a powerful empire in West Africa.

Bida In Soninke mythology, the giant snake that guarded Wagadu until it was killed by Mamadi.

Blue Men Term used for Tuareg men because of the stained blue dye on their faces. The dye comes off the scarves they wear to cover their faces.

Chameleon In Igbo mythology, was summoned by Chukwu to defeat Mermaid in a duel to see who was the best dressed god.

chi An Igbo personal god or guardian spirit.

Chukwu In Igbo mythology, he taught Nri how to grow the first crops. He was also challenged by Mermaid to see who was the better dressed of the two gods.

Dausi A series of epic poems or grand stories sung by Soninke griots.

Eri In Igbo mythology, the first man on Earth, sent down from heaven by Chukwu.

Eshu A Yoruba trickster god.

fa In Fon religion, the term for divination, or religious foresight.

griots West African chroniclers and storytellers.

Gu The god of iron, one of the Fon *vodun*.

Hawudui A spirit who, with Nyandebo, attended the Sande masquerade, met a girl, and allowed her to return with him to the heavens. There she chose a box, but when her father opened it, all the fierce creatures of the world were unleashed.

Hevioso A thunder god, one of the Fon *vodun*.

Ifa In Yoruba mythology, the Prince of Heaven, also called Orunmila, and the eldest son of Olorun. He instructed Obatala on how to create Ife.

Ife An ancient city now called Ile-Ife. In Yoruba mythology, it was created by Obatala, who named the place in honor of Orunmila (Ifa).

Iyadola In Igbo mythology, a spirit woman created by Nyame. She made the first humans out of clay.

kente A patterned cloth, often embroidered with gold threads, that was originally the dress of Ashanti kings and is now the national costume of Ghana.

keta Similar to *kente*, a cloth made by the Ewe of Togo and Ghana.

Kiloko In Soninke mythology, the buzzard that retrieved Tabele from the sky.

Lagarre Son of Mama Dinga, he made Wagadu visible.

Legba In Fon mythology, both a trickster god and the messenger of the *vodun*.

loa Haitian version of Fon *vodun*, or deities.

Maghegh A powerful jinni who was the father of the Tuareg people.

Mama Dinga An old king of Soninke whose son Lagarre made Wagadu visible.

Mamadi Sefe Dekote The killer of Bida and rescuer of Sia Jatta Bari. After he killed the giant snake, the people of Wagadu turned on him and he was forced to flee.

Mami-wata Also called Mother of Water, a popular god, or *vodu*, in both Africa and the Americas.

Mansa Musa Emperor of Mali in the early fourteenth century and one of its greatest rulers.

marabouts Muslim holy men of great learning who were believed to have supernatural powers.

Mawu-Lisa In Fon mythology, the creator of the universe and the mother of Sagbata and Sogbo.

Mermaid An Igbo goddess who challenged Chukwu.

Namuaku In Igbo mythology, the first woman and the wife of Eri.

Nri In Igbo mythology, Eri's eldest son. Chukwu taught him how to grow the first yams, cocoyams, oil palm, and breadfruit. He was also the founder of the Umunri people and the Nri dynasty.

Nyame In Igbo mythology, the Sky God who created all the animals (except humans) and plants on Earth.

Nyandebo A spirit who, with Hawudui, attended the Sande masquerade, met a girl, and allowed her to return with him to the heavens. There she chose a battered box containing riches.

Obatala In Yoruba mythology, a god who created the city of Ife.

ogwu-ji Yam medicine, which ensures a good harvest for Nri people.

Olokun In Yoruba mythology, the goddess of the empty waters.

Olorun In the Yoruba religion, the ruler of the gods.

oni Title given to a ruler of Ife.

orisha The Yoruba name for a god.

Sagbata In Fon mythology, the brother of Sogbo and the ruler of Earth's *vodun*.

Seku Ahmadu The first Muslim ruler of Masina, who asked Allah to trick Waada Samba.

seven Gaawo virgins In Tuareg mythology, the ancestral mothers of the Tuareg people.

Sia Jatta Bari A beautiful girl who lived in Wagadu and was to be sacrificed to Bida. She was rescued by Mamadi Sefe Dekote.

Sogbo In Fon mythology, the brother of Sagbata and the ruler of thunder, lightning, rain, and storms.

Sultan of Air Title of the ruler of the Tuareg.

Sundiata Founder of the Mali.

Sunni Ali Fifteenth-century ruler of the Songhay empire.

Tabele In a Soninke myth, the war drum that made Wagadu visible.

Tyi-wara A god—half man, half antelope—who taught the Bambara people how to farm.

vodun In Fon religion, the deity children of Mawu-Lisa, each controlling a different aspect of the world. A single one is called *vodu*.

Waada Samba A non-Muslim priest who used his jinni to help him answer Seku Ahmadu's challenge.

Wagadu A Soninke city that could magically appear and disappear.

Wututu The messenger bird of Sogbo who helped stop the fight between Sagbata and Sogbo and enabled the drought to end.

Further Information

BOOKS

Aardema, Verna, and Lisa Desimini. *Anansi Does the Impossible: An Ashanti Tale*. New York, NY: Aladdin, 2000.

Arkhurst, Joyce Cooper. *The Adventures of the Spider: West African Folktales*. Boston, MA: Little, Brown & Co., 1992.

Curtin, Philip D., ed. *Africa Remembered: Narratives by West Africans from the Era of the Slave Trade*. Prospect Heights, IL: Waveland Press, 1997.

Falola, Toyin. *The History of Nigeria*. Westport, CT: Greenwood Publishing Group, 1999.

Jeffrey, Gary. *African Myths*. New York, NY: Rosen Publishing Group, 2006.

VIDEOS

African Healing Dance. Sounds True Video, 1998.

In Search of History: Voodoo Secrets. A&E Video, 2000.

Sahara: A Place of Extremes. PBS Home Video, 2000.

WEB SITES

African Mythology
   http://www.mythencyclopedia.com/A-Am/African-Mythology.html

African Mythology
   http://www.godchecker.com/pantheon/african-mythology.php

West African Mythology
   http://www.windows.ucar.edu/tour/link=/mythology/african_culture.html

West African Myths

Index

Page numbers in *italics* refer to picture captions

Agadez 17
age-grade 32
alafins 36
Algeria 14, 16
Allah 19
Anansi 26–27, 28, 29
Arabs 8, *9*, 16
Aro 33
Ashanti 9, 29, 40, 41
Ashantihene 29
Askia Muhammad 21
Atlantic Ocean 20, 24

Bambara 9, 18, 45
Benin 22, 25, 36, 37
Berbers 9, 16
Bida 10, 11
Brazil 24
breadfruit 31, 32
Brer Bear 29
Brer Fox 29
Brer Rabbit 29
Brer Wolf 29
British 29, 33

Cameroon 8
Caribbean 24, 26
Chameleon 38, *39*, 40
chi 33
Christianity 5, *43*
Chukwu 30, 31, 33, 38, 40
clay children 6, 8
cloth 40, 41
cocoyams 30, 32
Congo River 9

Dausi 10, 12
diviners 22
Djenne *21*
Dogon *44*

Earth Mother *see* Iyadola
Edo 37
Eri 30
Eshu 28, 37
Europeans 8
Ewe 40

fa 22
Fang 9
Fon 22, 24, 25, 28, 41
Freetown *43*
Fulani 9, 41

Gaawo 14
Gabon 9
Gao 21
Gelede 45
Ghana 12, *13*, 21, 26, 29, 40
gold 10, 11, 17, 21, 29, 34, 40
griots 12, 13
Gu 25
Guinea 20
guinea fowl 18, 19

Haiti 24, 25
Hare 28, 29
Harris, Joel Chandler 29
Hausa 9
Hawudui 42, 43
Hevioso 25

Ibadan 36, 37
Ifa 34, 36
Ife 34, 36, 37
Ife-Ife 34, 36
Igbo 5, 6, 8, 28, 30, 32–33, 38
Ilorin 36, 37
Islam 5, 14, 18, 20, *43*
Iyadola 6–7, 8

jinni, jinn 10, 14, 15, 18

Kangaba 21
kente 40
keta 40, 41
Kiloko 10, *11*

Lagarre 10, 12
Legba 25, 28
Libya 14, 16, 17
loa 25

Macina 18, 20
Maghegh 15, 16
Mali 8, 13, 14, 16, 18, 20, *44*, 45
Malinke 9
Mama Dinga 10
Mamadi Sefe Dekote 11
Mami-wata 25
Mande languages 9
Mandingo 9, 21
mangrove *8*
Mansa Musa 21
marabouts 14, 18, 19
masquerades 41, 42, 44–45
Mauritania 8, 9
Mawu-Lisa 22, 25
Mende 9, *43*
Mermaid 38, 40
Moors 9
Morocco 21
mosque *21*
Mossi 40
Muhammad 14
Muslim 14, 17, 18, *21*

Namuaku 30
Niger 8, 14, 16, 20
Nigeria 9, 17, 20, 30, 34, 36, 37, 41
Niger River 9, 20, 21
nomads 16
Nri 30, 31, 32
Nyame 6, 7
Nyandebo 42

Obatala 34, 35
Oduduwa 36
Ogun 37
ogwu-ji 31
Olokun 34, *35*, 37, 38
Olorun 34, 36, 37, 38
oni 36
orishas 28, 37
Orunmila 34, 36
Oyo 36, 37

Poro 45
praise songs 12

raffia 41
rubber man 27

Sagbata 22, 23, 24
Sahara Desert *9*, 14, *15*, 16, 17, 21
Sahel 14
Sande 42, 45
Seku Ahmadu 18, 19, 20
Shango 37
Sia Jatta Bari 10, 11
Sierra Leone 40, 42, *43*, 45
sky-food 30
Sky God *see* Nyame
slaves 24–25
Sogbo 22, 23, 24, 25
Songhay 13, 18, 20, 21
Soninke 10, 12
Sultan of Air 17
Sundiata 21
Sunni Ali 21
Susu 21

Tabele 10
tagelmusts 17
termite mound 30, *31*
terra-cotta 37
Timbuktu 21
Togo 36, 40
Tortoise 28
tricksters 26, 28–29, 37
Tuareg 9, 14, 15, 16, 17
Tyi-wara 45

Uncle Remus: His Songs and His Sayings 29

vodun 22, 25
voodoo 24–25

Waada Samba 18
Wagadu 10, 11, 12
Wututu 22, 23

yams 30–31, 32
Yoruba 5, 9, 24, 28, 34, *35*, 36–37, 38, 40, 45